GUT DECISION

JEFF CARSON

GUT DECISION
A DAVID WOLF SHORT STORY

By Jeff Carson
http://jeffcarson.co
jeff@jeffcarson.co

Published by
Cross Atlantic Publishing

Sign up for the newsletter to stay up to date with new books at jeffcarson.co/p/newsletter.html.

CHAPTER 1

DEPUTY DAVID WOLF bounced in the seat of the truck as they barreled over the rut that split the earth between the asphalt and dirt road.

"I'm sorry, Wolf. I just had to do it," Deputy Sergeant Ryan Kazinsky said over the shaking SUV, which sounded like all the plastic in the cab was going to rattle off its screws. Kazinsky looked over at Wolf and shrugged. "I'm lookin' out for my ass, too, you know?"

Wolf blinked and nodded, unsure if the gesture was readable on top of the way he moved in the seat. He grabbed the Jesus bar and held his breath as they thumped over two potholes that looked like grenade craters.

"Damn, when are they gonna grade this shit?" Kazinsky looked over at Wolf.

Kazinsky was in his mid-thirties, just about ten years older than Wolf, but he looked younger than his years. His face was chubby and hairless, and he had big blue eyes with active blonde eyebrows. His hair was light blond, almost bleached-looking, and stuck straight up like a toothbrush.

It was the way he looked that made him seem young, but it was also the way he acted, the way he wore his emotions on the outside, Wolf thought. Take now for instance—Kazinsky was still looking at him. Incredulous. Leaning toward Wolf with his eyebrows popped up and eyes wide, like Wolf had had something to do with the terrible conditions of the road. Like Wolf was in on the conspiracy.

Wolf shrugged.

"Oh yeah," Kazinsky said, finally looking at the road and jerking the wheel to correct their trajectory. "You probably wouldn't know. You'd think by late June they'd have this road smoothed out from melt-season, though."

They rode in silence for a while, and Wolf looked out his window at the passing pine trees. Scrub oaks squatted on the orange and brown pebbly soil, surrounded by lush grasses that looked like if a match was thrown on them it would simply go out.

There was little dust being kicked up behind them. Another month and things would probably be parched, underbrush brittle and the grass brown, scratching the trunks of the trees like matchsticks. But this June had been wet so far, and that was following a rainy spring. The forest looked more like the ones he'd seen at Fort Lewis in Washington during his time in the army, rather than the Central Rockies.

They drove through a meadow blooming with white and pink flowers and the break in the trees revealed a sky darkening to a deep black behind the peaks.

"So?" Kazinsky glanced between the road and Wolf.

"So what, sir?"

"So I said I'm sorry."

"Yes, sir." Wolf nodded at Kazinsky. "No big deal. I get it. I've got some proving to do, sir."

Kazinsky lifted a hand and then gripped the wheel again. "I mean, you pointed your gun at a kid. It was a kid with a toy gun. That's like the type of crap you see on the news—cop shoots kid for carrying a toy gun—it's like the equivalent of a cop urban legend or something."

Wolf resumed looking out of his window. It had been a BB gun, but Wolf wasn't going to split hairs.

"I was told to tell Burton about anything that might concern me," Kazinsky said.

"Did he tell you to tell everyone else?" Wolf felt his face go flush the instant the words came out of his mouth. He kept his focus steady on the meadow.

Kazinsky didn't reply. Then he ran over another pothole, probably because he was triple- and quadruple-taking Wolf rather than concentrating on the road.

Wolf took a deep breath, regretting his outburst more with every passing second. Kazinsky was a transplant from the east coast, moving to Rocky Points sometime when Wolf had been in the army, so Wolf had no idea who the man was or what he was about, and so far he felt like he'd done nothing but put his worst foot forward so far.

Wolf sat back and let the tense silence grip them once again. He was getting used to it by now. He'd felt that same awkward quiet with every single member of the department since he'd returned from the academy and walked inside department headquarters, and then proceeded to do the dumbest thing he could have possibly done in his first week on patrol. He felt like he'd been kicked out of a club, thrown out on his face, and, now that he was outside, the doorman wasn't budging.

He watched the early afternoon sun go behind a cloud and let the scenario unfold in his mind for the thousandth time.

He'd been with Kazinsky on a dirt road much like this one, but on the other side of the valley where it was more populated. Wolf and Kazinsky had pulled over and gotten out, checking on a civilian who was just getting done changing a flat tire, when Wolf had heard the unmistakable crunch of feet on pine cones coming from the forest behind them.

When Wolf had seen the gun, he'd twisted and knelt down, all while pulling his gun clear of his holster and pointing it. In that same instant, he knew he'd overreacted, and he holstered his weapon with lightning speed.

But the damage had already been done, because Kazinsky and the civilian near his hobbled vehicle had seen everything. They'd watched a deputy no more than a week into training aim his newly issued Glock 17 at a ten-year-old boy named Jonathon Kenast, who had been walking out of the woods carrying an undersized plastic BB gun.

In Wolf's defense: it had been Wolf's third week on the job after graduating the Denver Police Academy (with flying colors), his first week out on patrol with another deputy of the Sluice County Sheriff's Department, and ten months after his sixth and final tour of duty in the 75th Ranger Battalion, where he'd shot and killed at least three kids younger than Jonathon in various places around the world—shots he'd taken that had ensured a lot of other people were still alive today, including Wolf himself.

In the kid's defense: Jonathon was no more than twenty yards from his house, playing in the trees just off a lawn that had been strewn with various other toys—plastic swords, other plastic guns, plastic knives—that should have tipped Wolf off that little boys were likely to be playing in the area. Also in the kid's defense: the BB gun was a light-gray spring-loader that dented pop cans rather than put holes in them.

Jonathon hadn't even seen what Wolf had done. He'd been busy concentrating on his cans, which had toppled off a log.

But Kazinsky had seen it, and so had the civilian. And now everyone in the department was avoiding Wolf, treating him like he had a highly contagious disease. All the deputies except Derek Connell, that is.

"Don't shoot any kids today, Wolf," Connell had said this morning when they'd left the station.

Now Kazinsky was finally getting around to apologizing to Wolf, as it was obvious he'd been reporting to more people than Sheriff Burton on Wolf's progress in training.

Wolf looked over at Kazinsky again.

Kazinsky was concentrating on the road, swerving around bumps and holes with unblinking eyes.

Wolf wanted to explain that he'd seen children in Sri Lanka wearing backpack-bombs with their thumbs on the trigger, that he'd seen AK-47-toting children in Afghanistan open fire into swarms of women and other children ... but explaining all that after aiming at a kid with a BB gun in an up-and-coming ski-resort town in the mountains of Colorado just made Wolf look like an even worse-looking candidate for a sheriff's deputy. He looked skittish because he was.

Explaining the messed-up reasons for it would only serve to make him look more so.

So Wolf looked back out the window and kept his lips shut, an approach he'd been taking for the last few days since the incident.

Sheriff Burton had accepted Wolf's silence so far. Sure, Burton had sat Wolf down in his sauna-like office and stared at him for what seemed like five minutes without blinking, but Burton had not demanded an explanation. Instead, he'd just glared. Thinking. Evaluating.

Wolf felt a bead of sweat now form on his forehead as he thought about it, because Burton had put himself on the line, hiring Wolf without an interview. Wolf had ridden into the department on the coattails of his father's reputation, and now everyone was rearing their heads up, wondering just what kind of crazy, broken young man the sheriff had allowed in.

Kazinsky cleared his throat, giving Wolf a sympathetic glance. "Just don't worry about Connell. He's a hothead, likes to rile people up."

"So I remember," Wolf said.

"Oh yeah, you went to school with him, didn't you?"

Wolf nodded. "We've been in the same school, same classes for most of our lives. He hasn't changed since the day in the third grade when he moved here. We've always gotten into it, and something tells me things won't be changing soon."

CHAPTER 2

"So where'd you live growing up?" Kazinsky turned down the screaming Pink Floyd guitar solo to a whisper.

Wolf pointed to the south. "Out of town to the southeast, on a ranch along the Chatauqua."

Kazinsky nodded. "Oh, nice. I think I've seen that place."

"Has bull horns on the archway," Wolf said. "Bull Creek, that's what my dad used to call it before he died."

Kazinsky went quiet for a beat. "You live there now?"

Wolf nodded.

"You're married, though, right?"

Wolf nodded again.

Kazinsky got the hint and stopped his line of questioning.

Wolf cleared his throat. "How about you? Where are you from in Vermont?"

"Place called Woodstock."

"Ah." Wolf nodded, wondering why today was their first attempt to talk about anything but the job in over a week. Maybe Kazinsky felt bad, felt like he'd gone behind his partner's back by telling everyone about his mistake and was trying to make up for it by being personable.

Wolf kept his eyes out the window, watching Sandy Creek flit in and out of view behind the trees. There were a few fishermen out in the middle of the waist-deep water, tossing lines and concentrating on their hooks.

Two pickup trucks, parked on the side of the road, came into view ahead.

Kazinsky slowed to a crawl as they passed, and squinted out the windshield. "Those plates current?"

Wolf leaned forward and peered down. "Yep."

Kazinsky slowed at the next pickup, asked the same question and got the same answer from Wolf.

"We don't check their fishing licenses ever, right?" Wolf asked.

"Not unless you want to." Kazinsky turned up the radio a little, just in time for the end of the song.

They drove without talking for a while, all the while Wolf wondering if other deputies in the department were doing the same thing right now—wandering back roads, miles from the center of the only respectably populated town in the county, searching for the occasional expired plate on fishermen's trucks, waiting for something to come out of the woods and bite them.

Surely there was more to it all, Wolf thought. But then again, they did live in a sleepy ski-resort town, in a tiny sliver-like county in the middle of the Rocky Mountains.

Wolf shook his head. For every passing moment of absolutely nothing happening, Wolf found it even more incredible that he'd managed to make such a mess of his situation.

Wolf locked eyes with the radio as it made a loud scratching noise. "523, do you have a copy?"

Kazinsky lazily flipped the music off and plucked the radio from the dash unit. "Copy, go ahead."

"We've got a report of a disturbance at 193 McCall Mountain Road."

Kazinsky rolled his eyes at the ceiling. "Shhhhhhhit, you've gotta be ..." He put the radio up to his mouth and pushed the button. "Are you saying the disturbance is being reported by someone else?"

"Negative, 523." The husky female voice of Tammy Granger sounded amused. "I'm checking my notes here, and you're next up on the rotation."

Kazinsky blew air through his lips. "We're on our way."

Wolf watched Kazinsky hook the radio back on the dash. "What was that all about?"

Kazinsky slowed and turned around the SUV. "That was what we call a waste of tax-payer money. We are on our way to a well-known address—"

"Don't shoot her," a voice came from the radio.

Kazinsky looked over at Wolf and then at the radio, then back out the windshield. "There's a crazy lady who lives at this address. She calls us at least three times a week"—he shook his head—"Goddamn nightmare."

"And what? Nothing ever legitimately wrong?" Wolf kept his eyes conspicuously away from the radio.

"Never."

"Never?"

"Never. It's my fourth year in the department, and I've been to her house countless times, and there's never anything. Gotta go, though. It's our job. Our duty. She uses the vandalism card a lot. Then she'll say she has bears trying to get into her house ... let's see, what else? One time she said a crackhead was trying to get onto her property. A crackhead. Apparently just wandering around the forests of the Rocky Mountains. This is kind of a new one, though. Disturbance. But that could just be Tammy's term. I guess we'll find out."

CHAPTER 3

THEY DROVE BACK down the road to the asphalt and Kazinsky really opened up the engine. After a couple white-knuckle minutes, they reached 734 and hung a left into town. Once the highway turned into Main Street, they passed the Mackery Gas Station on the right, then slowed and took a right on County 23, another dirt road otherwise known as Wildflower Road.

The houses nearest town were small and squat-looking, compact in their designs, where ski bums working at the mountain lived with five other roommates during the ski season. As they drove higher up the road, the houses thinned out and grew bigger, with more copper and stone, more wood stain instead of brown paint. There were no potholes on the road, and no rocks poking up out of nowhere. It was smooth, well maintained.

Wolf hadn't been on the road since coming back from the army, but he recognized where they were going, and knew the road well.

"She lives in these houses?" he asked.

Kazinsky nodded with raised eyebrows.

"That's so strange," Wolf said.

"That she could be so psychotic and live in such a nice neighborhood?" Kazinsky asked. "Yeah. Not sure how that happened."

They slowed at a red street sign with white writing that said McCall Mountain Road, named after one of the peaks on the eastern side of the valley, which was in perfect view out of Wolf's passenger window. They hung a right turn.

The road was much more populated than Wolf had remembered it. New houses had sprung up from the forest on either side. They were large, but not outlandishly so, like many of the other homes he remembered that were higher up County 23. These houses hunkered back from the road, each sitting on a couple of acres of flat pine forest, with rocky drives in front, carpeted with natural grasses and flowers between trees, with slivered views of the surrounding mountains.

Wolf looked in the side-view mirror and caught a glimpse of the grassy slopes of the ski resort to the south.

This was the type of place he wanted to move into with Sarah and Jack.

That was, if he could keep his job. And, that was, if he could keep his wife.

Thinking of Sarah made him swallow. Ever since he'd been home from the academy, she'd changed big time. Sarah's mother had mentioned post-partum depression, and Wolf suspected that was true, but he also suspected another culprit, because he'd seen it happening long before the last few months. It had started well before he'd come home for good, and well before Jack's birth.

He had it nailed to his visit home after his third tour. He remembered how her once tropical-sea-blue eyes had faded to a more pallid shade, and how they had been spider-webbed with veins around the edges.

Her personality had taken a nose-dive, too, like she'd been concentrating on something else every time he tried to talk to her.

It was drugs. None of the hard stuff, but of the prescription variety, which Wolf knew could become just as bad, just as life altering, as any other addiction. Wolf was positive about it now. He'd read up on the symptoms, and a little asking around town in the right places had all but confirmed it for him.

He and Sarah still had a fighting chance, though. He just needed to solidify this job, the job he'd decided he wanted to do for the rest of his life, the job his father had done before him so well, and then he'd worry about bringing his wife back up the dangerous hill she'd been sliding down without a rope. Then maybe in a few years they could move up here.

"Here we go," Kazinsky said, slowing the SUV in front of a wooded, flat driveway that was a couple of grooves with a stripe of green grass in the middle. At the end of it was a nice-looking pine log house with tall windows and flowerpots on the front porch.

The truck swayed as they drove onto the ruts.

Wolf gripped the bar on the ceiling again as the pine trees shot past at high speed.

Kazinsky scraped to a stop in the gravel drive and a woman came out of the door on cue. Kazinsky stepped out, and the woman walked up to him with purpose.

Wolf stepped around the SUV and joined them as they

squared off like two fighters in a ring before the bell—Kazinsky looking down with a puffed chest and thumbs on his duty belt, the woman looking up at him with a defiant glare.

Wolf stopped a few feet away and studied the woman. She was dressed in a dark pair of jeans and a leathery-looking shirt with tassels, and wore Birkenstock sandals on her feet. A long strap with a beaded sack hung around her neck, and most of her fingers were adorned with silver rings.

She had long gray hair, pulled back in a loose ponytail. The skin on her face was fuzzy and wrinkled, and her eyes were squinted, her face contorted like she was sucking on a sour candy as she looked up at Kazinsky.

She peaked her hands in front of her. "Listen, Deputy. I want to tell you about—"

"How are you today, Mrs. Addison?" Kazinsky asked.

"—a noise I heard in the forest earlier. It's not something I've heard before. It's not a normal sound one would expect to hear from the forest, I can tell you that. It was more a—"

"Don't you want to meet the new deputy?" Kazinsky waved a hand over at Wolf.

"—scream. No, a shriek. An animal dying a horrific death perhaps? A person in danger, a female person in danger, screaming because an animal has attacked her? Making her frail and helpless and afraid?"

"Well, we haven't had any other calls, Mrs. Addison. When do you say you heard this ... noise?"

She squinted harder and pointed her index finger up at Kazinsky. "A shriek, or a scream. We pay you people good money with our tax dollars to take care of problems like these, so I would appreciate it if you do not treat me as a problem when I ask that you check in on things like this. These incidences up here plague our community."

Kazinsky looked over at Wolf. "You sure you don't want to ..."—he bounced his eyebrows and flicked a few glances at Wolf's gun—"... no? You sure?"

Wolf stared at Kazinsky.

"What was that?" She looked over at Wolf. "What are you doing?" She looked down at Wolf's gun, then back up at him.

Wolf shot Kazinsky a glare, backed up, walked around the SUV, opened the door, and got in.

He sat quietly, watching them through the windows, and he heard her talk about a Disney movie, and then the maliciousness of the neighbor's cat, and then Wolf didn't bother following any more of the conversation.

A few minutes later, Wolf opened his eyes at the sound of the car door opening.

"Damn it," Kazinsky said, climbing into his seat. "She's a piece of work. What's the matter, you didn't want to stick around?"

Wolf shook his head. "Yeah, right. You had me headed in a good direction there. Thanks."

Kazinsky laughed heartily as he shifted into drive and screamed back up the driveway.

Wolf couldn't help but smile, and was grateful for a little hazing to his face rather than suspicion and murmurs behind his back.

At the end of the driveway, Kazinsky took a left and looked over at Wolf.

"You know, just stay cool. This'll all blow over. Burton likes you, that's clear enough. Just because Connell is being

Connell doesn't mean everybody else is feeling the same way."

Wolf nodded. "Thanks."

They drove down the road and Wolf looked out his window at the passing houses. They varied in size and age; some built over twenty years ago and others still unfinished.

As they passed another gap in the trees, he leaned towards the glass to get a better look at the next house. This was an older one with two stories and a two-car garage. There were three windowed gables on the upper level, so it was probably a three or four bedroom. He wondered what the price tag was for one of these.

He looked to the rear of the house, and saw that it backed to a gentle sloping forest; much like their ranch house his father had built years ago.

He looked up at the window on the end and saw a little girl's face pressed to the glass. It was definitely a perfect house for a family. Wolf could picture going out with Jack in the woods to shoot BB guns, maybe teach him how to throw a knife.

Wolf locked eyes with the girl in the window for a moment, and then his breath caught. Because as they stared at one another through the passing lodge pole pines, he watched her open her mouth and clench her eyes shut, like she was yelling at the top of her lungs, and then she pressed her palm against the window.

Then there was movement behind her, and her face backed away from the window with wrenching speed, but her palm remained. Then there was another movement in the darkness beyond the glass, and her palm was gone.

"Stop!" Wolf kept his eyes glued to the swaying drapes as they relaxed to cover the window.

Kazinsky slowed. "What? What the hell?"

"Stop."

The SUV continued down the road.

Wolf glared at Kazinsky. "Pull over. I just saw something."

Kazinsky shook his head as they rumbled to a stop. "What?"

"I saw a little girl pressed up against the window of that last house. She was screaming, and then someone pulled her away. She looked like she was in trouble. Maybe Mrs. Addison actually heard something this time."

Kazinsky took a deep breath and glanced in the rearview mirror. "Okay, so ..." He shook his head again and shifted into reverse.

"Wait," Wolf said. "Let's just walk back, see what we can see on the way."

Kazinsky stared at him for a few seconds with his hand on the shifter. Keeping his eyes locked on Wolf's, he put it in park, switched off the engine, and then turned and got out.

Wolf got out and shut the door. The air was still and cool, shaking lightly as a rumble of thunder came from the darkening clouds overhead.

Wolf kicked up a few grasshoppers as he crunched through the weeds. The SUV ticked and hissed, smelling of hot rubber. He met Kazinsky at the rear of the SUV and stopped.

"Are you serious?" Kazinsky stared at Wolf with relaxed eyes. It was a warning and a question at the same time.

"I know what I saw." Wolf lifted his chin.

Kazinsky stared for another few seconds and held out his hand for Wolf to lead.

Wolf turned away and started walking down the dirt road.

Unseen insects hummed everywhere, and then they suddenly stopped, plunging the deputies into silence except for the scraping of their boot falls.

Wolf slowed as a slice of the house came into view through the forest. He held up a hand and stopped, and Kazinsky slapped it away and continued by him.

Wolf watched Kazinsky march down the road, kicking rocks in front of him like a kid walking to school.

Wolf looked back to the house and picked out the window again. The cream-colored drapes hung still.

Wolf jogged to catch up to Kazinsky and then stepped alongside him.

"See anything?" Kazinsky asked, looking into the forest on the other side of the road.

Wolf didn't answer. He was studying the window and the rest of the house as they walked. An American flag mounted on one of the front porch posts swayed gently on a stick. The house siding was painted dark blue, and though it was set back away from the road, Wolf could see details, and could tell it was dirty, with brown smears on the paint that had built up over years of no cleaning.

The open space of land in front of the house was overgrown with wispy grass and littered with years' worth of pinecone accumulation. There was a pink and white plastic slide, and upon further inspection there were a few other children's toys scattered about—a plastic bucket and shovel, a small bicycle leaning up against the side of the house, a doll lying on its back.

They stopped at the plunging turn-off to the gravel driveway.

Kazinsky squinted and put his hands on his hips, appraising the house. "I don't see shit, Wolf."

Wolf took a deep breath and pulled his duty belt up off his hipbone, careful to keep his hand away from his gun. There was no sound, no movement of any kind, no sign that anyone was home.

"Up there," Wolf said. "In the furthest right window on top. I saw a little girl scream."

Kazinsky twisted towards Wolf. "Do you know who lives here?"

Wolf looked over at Kazinsky and narrowed his eyes. "No, sir. Who?"

"Name's Brady. He owns Rascal's Dry Cleaners and Rascal's Hardware."

Wolf nodded. "Oh. Yeah, I know the guy. So?"

"So he's a guy who knows a lot of people in town. A respected businessman, connections with the county council, probably. And the county council? You've gotta learn that they have the power in this town."

"He has kids?" Wolf asked.

Kazinsky smiled and shook his head, like Wolf was beyond help. "He's older. Has kids and grandkids, I think."

Wolf nodded and then walked down the driveway. After a few steps he heard Kazinsky following him.

As he neared the house, Wolf could see that there were spider webs in the cracks of the siding. The tiny pink steps to the plastic slide in front were caked with dirt and more webs. The slide itself was thick with dirt and debris.

There was a crack of thunder, followed by a long rumble. Darkness seemed to push down on them from above.

Three steps led up to a wooden porch that extended the entire length of the house in front. There was a swinging chair hanging from rusty chains on the right and nothing but dust and pine needles off to the left.

Wolf walked up, and the gray boards creaked underneath his boots. The front door was dented and scratched, smudged in black on the bottom like it was usually opened with a twist of the knob and a swift kick. He pushed the doorbell and a dingdong sound came from inside.

Kazinsky stopped next to him with crossed arms, looking at Wolf with raised eyebrows.

There was a long silence, and then faint footsteps inside; they got nearer, and then they stopped. Wolf and Kazinsky looked at each other. A latch clicked on the door, and then another, and then another.

The door creaked open to reveal a little girl looking up with wide eyes. She wore a pink long-sleeved shirt with unicorns on it, and pink pants; on her feet were white socks with lace fringes. Her hair was blonde and pulled back in a ponytail.

Wolf didn't recognize her as the girl he'd just seen, but he could have been mistaken. Maybe if she started screaming she'd be the spitting image.

Instead she wore no expression at all, standing board-straight and still.

"Hi," Wolf said. "How are you to—"

The door opened up further and a smiling man, gray and

older in his years loomed tall. "Hello, Officers ... er, sorry, Deputies. What's going on?"

Wolf looked over at Kazinsky, and Kazinsky was looking back at him with intense curiosity.

"Uh, hello, sir. My name is Deputy Wolf. This is Deputy Sergeant Kazinsky. We're with the sheriff's department"—he paused, and when the other man didn't offer his name, Wolf felt his face flush—"I was ... we were just driving by ... we had a report of a girl screaming in the vicinity. We were wondering if you'd heard anything."

The man's eyes lit up and he chuckled. "I hear screaming all the time with this little one."

Wolf looked down at the girl. She was blinking rapidly— hard, prolonged blinks, like she had Tourette's syndrome or was fighting a nervous tick. She was scratching her chest with her index finger, like she was trying to scrape a spot off her shirt that wasn't there.

"Uh," Wolf said, staring intently at the girl for another moment. The man placed a large hand on the girl's shoulder.

She twisted her head and looked up at the man with a smile that was all mouth and no eyes.

"Is this your daughter, sir?" Wolf asked.

The man chuckled again. "No, no. At my age?"

Wolf felt a calm wash over him as he stared into the man's eyes. It was the calm he'd felt countless times in battle, when he knew his targets were all accounted for and in range.

The man stared back with a relaxed gaze. His eyes were glacier blue, set deep in hooded eyelids underneath unkempt gray bushes for eyebrows. His ashen hair was slicked back, clumped in solid strips, held in place with some sort of pomade.

"It's my granddaughter," the man said, looking over at Kazinsky and then down at Wolf's uniform. He squinted and then popped his bushel eyebrows up. "Oh, you're Deputy Wolf? Your father, I knew him growing up. He was a good man. I was sorry to hear about his passing."

Wolf nodded. "Thank you, sir. What's your name?"

Kazinsky shifted his weight. Wolf could see in his periphery that Kazinsky was staring at him, much like Superman did before lasers shot out of his eyes.

"Brady," he said taking off his hand from the girl's shoulder and extending it. "James Brady."

Wolf grasped his hand and shook it. Brady had thick, rough skin and a firm grip—not painfully hard, not dead-squirrel soft, but with enough gusto to suggest he was a man to be counted on to step up to any challenge.

"Nice to meet you," Wolf said, stepping back a step and glancing down at the girl again.

She'd stopped her fidgeting and was looking at the boards of the porch.

"And how about you?" Wolf asked, looking at the top of the girl's head.

"This is Elizabeth." Brady rubbed her back again.

Elizabeth kept her eyes at Wolf's feet.

"Eh." Brady held up his hand and shook his head, like there was no helping Elizabeth from being so shy. "Hey, why don't you go back upstairs and play?" He rubbed her back again.

She looked up at Wolf and scratched her chest once more, and then disappeared back in the house.

Brady leaned to the side, ducking his head behind the door, and then he swayed back into view. "I've heard about you, you know." He nodded at Wolf. "About your tours in the army. I know what it's like. To come home after serving."

Brady leaned back inside. "Remember what I said, okay?" he said to someone behind the door.

There was no response from inside as Brady leaned back out with a shake of his head and a smile. "She's so cute, but so rambunctious."

Wolf nodded. "How many granddaughters do you have?"

"Just the one ... well, three, but just the one here."

Kazinsky cleared his throat. "Well, thanks Mr. Brady. That'll be all." He put a hand on Wolf's shoulder.

"Like I was saying," Brady said, ignoring Kazinsky, "I know what it's like coming home. Tough to assimilate to civilian life again, always thinking you're in a battle situation ... believe me, I know. I was at Hamburger Hill in Nam. When I came home"—he shook his head and stared into the past—"man, I was seein' gooks everywhere. I thought everyone was out to shoot me and my family ..."

Wolf looked down at the porch. "Thank you, sir. Let us know if you hear anything suspicious, will you?"

"Will do. And if you want to talk, come on in to the hardware store any time. I own Rascal's."

"Yes, I know that. Thank you, sir," Wolf said.

Wolf and Kazinsky walked off the porch, and Wolf gave a final look up to the drapes in the window. They were still.

"What the hell was that?" Kazinsky asked.

A cold drop of rain slapped the back of Wolf's neck.

"Shit." Kazinsky looked up at the sky and broke into a jog.

Wolf trotted behind him.

Just as they reached the SUV, the sky flashed and a

thunder followed a few seconds later. When they climbed in, a steady rain pelted the top of the truck. Then there was a loud smack on the roof above Wolf, and then another. White balls of hail started exploding on the windshield.

Kazinsky reached up and put the keys into the ignition.

Wolf put a hand on his arm. "You didn't see that?"

Kazinsky twisted the keys and the SUV rumbled to life. "What?"

"That girl."

"What? Yeah, I saw that girl. So what?"

"Don't do that." Wolf pointed at Kazinsky's hand on the gearshift. "Just a second."

Kazinsky removed his hand and twisted in the seat.

"When that girl was standing at the door," Wolf said, "she was giving us a signal. You didn't see that?"

Kazinsky frowned. "You mean she was twitching like she was a crack baby in her earlier life and scratching herself like she hadn't been bathed in a week? Yeah, I saw that. So what?"

"It was a pattern. She was blinking a pattern. It was SOS —three short blinks, three long blinks, three short blinks. Morse code."

Wolf did it to demonstrate, and when he opened his eyes for the last time, Kazinsky was staring at him differently.

Kazinsky's eyes involuntarily darted around the cab, like he was calculating his next move. *How am I going to calm this freak down without getting hurt?*

Wolf ignored his concern. "I watched her do it the first time, and then she repeated it when I looked at her again. And the way she was scratching her chest. Did you see that?

She was doing it with her index finger, and pointing up and to her left."

Kazinsky was incredulous. "What?"

"She was pointing upstairs. Where I saw the girl in the window."

"What? Oh, Jesus Christ. If there was a girl in the window, that was her! You just met her! And she looked just fine by me."

Wolf leaned back and closed his eyes. "No, sir. I don't think so. I think I saw a different girl in that window, and I think the girl at the front door was trying to say help. And I think Mrs. Addison heard something for real this time."

Kazinsky stared with an open mouth, and then closed it and swallowed. He looked in the rearview mirror, and then looked at the radio on the dash.

"Look," Wolf said, "did you see those toys out front? The slide? Nobody's been using those things for years. It's like they're props or something. They're caked with dirt."

"So let me just understand exactly what you are saying," Kazinsky said slowly. "You're saying two girls are in there, and James Brady, the owner of Rascal's Dry Cleaners and Rascal's Hardware, has ... kidnapped these two girls? Is holding that perfectly calm—I'll give you twitchy, fine, but perfectly calm—little girl in there?"

Wolf blinked.

"I have just a few questions for you." Kazinsky sniffed. "How old do you think that little girl you just met is?"

Wolf shrugged. "I don't know. Eight? Nine?"

"More like eight," Kazinsky said. "Let's say she's nine just for kicks. Screw it, let's say she's freaking ten years old. Do you think a ten-year-old girl is going to know Morse code?"

Wolf shook his head. "That girl didn't know Morse code. She knew Morse code for saying help. SOS. That's a simple pattern a three-year-old could master. Who knows what that little girl's background is? Her father could be military."

Kazinsky covered his eyes with his palms and rubbed. "One more question. One more. Do you think you might be seeing some things lately that aren't there? Like ... I don't know, the other day when you pulled your gun on a different kid who you thought was coming out of the woods like some sort of a guerilla-warfare attacker."

Wolf looked out the window.

"Goddammit!" Kazinsky yelled. "Now I gotta tell Burton about this! What the hell is your problem? Have you noticed that both these kids are about the same age? Does that mean something? Did something hap—"

"I know what I saw." Wolf pulled the door handle and stepped out into the steady rain. "Call for backup."

Kazinsky yanked the radio off the dash and stared at Wolf. "It's your ass."

"Do it."

Kazinsky smiled like he was now watching the funniest movie of the year. "Dispatch, do you have a copy? This is 523, I need—"

Wolf shut the door and walked. He angled his head down to block the rain from hitting his face, and it drenched his neck, running down his spine. He felt the skin all over his body pull into gooseflesh as he reached up and pinched his uniform collar closed.

CHAPTER 4

THE DOOR CLICKED THREE TIMES, and this time it only opened a sliver. One blue eye appeared, narrowed, glanced over Wolf's shoulder, then the door opened wider.

"Yes?" Brady said with a blank stare.

Wolf sighed and scratched his head. "Hi, uh ... Mr. Brady, sir. I'm sorry for bothering you again. I just ..." He let his sentence fade and craned his neck to peer past Brady, a move that caused Brady instinctively to narrow the opening. A move that told Wolf his instincts were right.

"I just wanted to speak to you about ... what we were just talking about. About coming back from the military."

Brady eyed him suspiciously. "Where's your partner?"

Wolf waved a dismissive hand to the rain. "He's in the vehicle. I told him I'd be back in a bit."

There was a thump from somewhere in the house. Wolf kept his eyes glued to Brady's, and Brady did the same with Wolf's.

"Anyways, I was just thinking—"

"Like I said, you can come into the hardware store any

time"—he looked down behind the door and then back to Wolf—"I've gotta get back to playtime. You have kids?"

Wolf nodded. "Yeah, actually I have a boy who's almost one year old."

Brady raised those caterpillars above his eyes and smiled. "Ah ... so you'll know soon enough. Kids this age can be so rowdy. They wrestle all day, and break things, jump off things. Oh my goodness, it's a nightmare."

Wolf tilted his head. "Wrestle? That's kind of a two-kid sport, right?"

Brady's Adam's apple traveled up and down his neck as he swallowed, and then he blinked. "We like to wrestle."

Wolf hardened his gaze.

Brady was clearly lying. The signs Wolf had learned in anti-interrogation training as a ranger, and again in the police academy, were all there—he swallowed, he broke eye-contact as he darted glances all over Wolf's uniform and then out into the rain, his skin flushed red, and he licked his lips.

Just then the sound of sirens pierced the air behind Wolf, and then there was the high-pitched whine of engines being floored and tires rumbling on the gravel road.

Wolf turned around and peered through the falling rain and dripping pines just as two SCSD vehicles came into view, lights flashing and sirens blaring.

He looked back at Brady and just barely kicked his foot out in time to keep the door from closing.

"Ah," Wolf cried as the slamming door folded his foot.

The sirens went quiet as tires scraped to a halt.

Wolf jumped forward, slamming his shoulder into the door as hard as he could. Wolf heard and felt a thud as the door connected solidly with Brady, and then there was no resistance on the door at all.

Wolf stumbled into the entryway of the house just in time to see Brady come to rest on the wood floor. He was stunned, but not unconscious.

More sirens came and silenced. More scratching halts of tires on dirt road. Wolf looked out the door and saw two deputies sprinting down the driveway with guns drawn.

"Freeze!" Connell's face was twisted in hatred as he screamed through clenched teeth. His legs pumped furiously, thumping through shallow puddles as he left another deputy trailing far behind. Deputy Baine, Wolf recognized with a glance.

Wolf watched the doors on the other vehicle open, and then he heard more sirens in the distance.

With a click, Wolf shut the door and muffled the noise outside.

It was quiet save a ticking clock on the wall and the whimpers of Brady on the floor. The air was warm and humid.

His whole body jolted when he finally took in the full situation. Brady was squirming on the ground, gripping his head with one hand and a television remote control in the other. Next to him, sprawled on her stomach, was the motionless body of the little girl dressed in pink.

He stepped over Brady and knelt down, putting his arm on her back. He was relieved when she twisted and whimpered.

Wolf felt dizzy for an instant. *What am I doing?*

He heard the footsteps getting closer outside, and he

jumped up and lunged for the door, latching two of the locks as fast as he could.

When he turned around he saw that Brady was sitting up, staring at Wolf with a half-smile. A few strands of hair were draped on his forehead, and he reached up and pushed them back with his hand.

The door thumped. "Let us in! Wolf! What are you doing?"

"I told you, it's hard to separate, son," Brady said, pointing the remote at him and bouncing it like a baton.

Wolf pulled his gun and looked straight ahead at a carpeted stairway that climbed five or so steps, turned ninety degrees to the left, and then rose to the second floor. "Don't you move."

Brady nodded once. *Yes, sir.*

Connell screamed again outside, and then the door was hit with a huge blow, shaking the floor.

Wolf stepped toward the girl named Elizabeth and patted her back.

She whined, and Wolf could see a growing mat of red hair on the back of her head. *Shit.*

With a jolt, she got onto all fours, coming to in the blink of an eye. "Help m—" She looked over at Brady and froze, and then she looked at Wolf.

"Do you need help?" Wolf asked.

She looked over at Brady. Brady stared at her with a grandfatherly look of concern.

"Elizabeth. Listen to me. Do you need help? It's okay. You can tell me."

The front door thumped harder than before and the wood frame splintered with a loud crack.

Wolf looked at Elizabeth's expressionless face again and then stood and sprinted up the stairs. Just as he reached the second floor, the front door crashed open below. As frantic footsteps filled the landing below, he ran down the hallway and saw a closed door with a sliver of natural light underneath.

He twisted the knob and it clicked open.

He held his breath and pushed the door. Then he exhaled and stepped inside. It was a stereotypical version of a girl's room—pink walls, a pink bed and bedspread with stuffed animals arranged just so, a pink desk with a red notebook on top of it, and a wooden chair with a princess painted on it—those things and more, and nothing else out of the ordinary.

Wolf dropped his hands by his side and stared in confusion. He threw his gun behind him and into the hallway as he heard the first deputy reach the door.

"Wolf," Connell said. "Turn around."

Wolf did.

Connell aimed his gun at Wolf's chest. Connell was twitching, his finger white on the trigger; his chest was heaving, his whole muscle-bound body pumped with adrenaline.

"Get down on the ground and put your hands behind your head." Connell's voice was deadly.

Wolf stood motionless, trying to remember every detail of the last minute. He'd missed something. He was sure of it.

"Wolf!" Connell lurched his pistol forward. Baine came up from behind Connell and saw Wolf's pistol on the ground.

"Easy, Connell. Wolf." Baine held up a hand.

"Shut up, Baine. I said get down on—"

"How many doors are in the hall outside?" Wolf nodded at Baine.

"I said turn around and get on your knees, right now!" Connell yelled.

"Baine, how many doors?" Wolf asked. "Are there two or—"

"Now! I'm warning you!"

Sheriff Burton crashed into the room and got in front of Baine. "Deputy, stand down!"

Connell looked over at Burton and stepped aside, keeping his gun trained on Wolf.

"Stand down." Burton held out his hand to Connell.

Wolf stood motionless, and the room went silent except for the panting of all four men.

"Take off your duty belt and throw it over here," Burton said.

Wolf shook his head. "Sir, I—"

"Do it. Or I'll tell Connell to shoot you in the leg."

Connell raised his gun again.

Wolf unbuckled his belt and threw it on the floor at Connell's feet.

Connell kicked it to the corner, knocking over a teddy bear leaning against the wall.

"Turn around," Burton said. "Put your hands behind your back."

Wolf did it.

Connell pressed the cuffs tight until the metal pinched bone. He shoved him out into the hall, slamming Wolf into a painting, which came off and fell at Wolf's feet.

"Connell," Burton warned.

"Sorry, sir."

Out in the hall, Wolf saw that the next bedroom was wide open. On the way by, he looked in and saw his suspicions confirmed.

"There are two doors here," Wolf said. "Two bedrooms. Two windows."

Nobody responded. Someone pushed him hard towards the stairway and he just stopped himself from tumbling over the banister and onto the landing far below. Wolf knew it was Connell, relishing every second, giving into his murderous instincts, knowing anyone would understand Connell's rage since Wolf had just knocked a girl bloody and unconscious.

As Wolf started down the steps he was thumped in the back. Wolf jumped down five steps, ending up on the landing that was halfway up the stairs, barely avoiding a serious crash into the wall straight ahead.

He turned to go down the rest of the stairs and saw that the entryway below was empty except for Kazinsky.

On the final step, Wolf was pushed from behind once again, but this time he couldn't get his feet underneath him and he landed hard on his shoulder and face.

Sergeant Kazinsky stared down, and waited impassively as Wolf struggled to get to his knees.

Wolf winced as someone yanked him up by the cuffs. He felt his bones stress to the point of cracking. His shoulder connected with the doorjamb on the way out to the porch.

"Connell," Burton warned, "no more."

Connell let go and Wolf walked out into the damp air.

Brady was standing on the porch next to two other deputies, staring into Wolf's eyes. He wasn't grinning anymore. He was glaring hard, like he despised Wolf with every cell of his body.

Or was it a look of warning?

The girl was a few feet away from Brady, staring back into the house, shuffling to get a better view.

It wasn't natural. A granddaughter that had just been knocked out by an intruder would have been cowering in her grandfather's arms.

"This guy is up to ..." Wolf stopped talking. He needed to show them.

As they reached the step off the front porch, Wolf stopped and moved to the side. He watched in the corner of his eye as Connell's arms whiffed past, and then he lunged back at Connell and connected with his shoulder.

Connell hit the post with the American flag, slipped on the wet wood, and went down hard.

Wolf trotted down the steps and out into the drizzle, and then turned and looked up at the house.

Burton, Kazinsky, and Baine were on him in a second.

"Up there," Wolf said as an arm wrapped around his neck. "Three ..."—the chokehold was tightening on his esophagus—"windows."

They wrestled him to the ground, and the water soaked through his uniform, chilling his back and legs.

"Wait." Burton looked up. "What? Let him up. Let him up!"

They scattered, leaving Wolf to roll himself onto his stomach, where he pressed his forehead onto the ground, got to his knees, and stood up.

Burton was volleying glances between the windows and Brady, who was now close to the girl, hand resting on her shoulder.

"It's the remote control!" the girl screamed at the top of

her lungs, pointing to Brady's hand as she walked towards them. "The remote control!"

While each and every sheriff's deputy stared dumbfounded at a girl frantically screaming about a cheap plastic piece of electronics, which may or may not have something to do with a window, Wolf understood. And Brady knew it.

For an instant they locked eyes, and at the same instant they both sprang into action—Brady going for the front door and Wolf going for Brady.

Wolf ran up the steps past Connell.

Brady stepped across the porch and into the house, all the while pointing the remote control up toward the window and pecking at it with his finger. Brady's lips were twisted in a snarl, as if he was shooting a hail of bullets out of the remote control rather than an invisible RF signal.

Hands still bound by the cuffs, Wolf had few options. He reared his foot back like an NFL punter and kicked up as hard as he could. As Wolf sailed back-first toward the threshold step of the doorway, he connected with his foot, and the bones of Brady's forearm tented upward with a sharp snap. The remote control dropped from his hand and spun in the air, and in that same instant Wolf landed awkwardly on his left side and felt a bone snap in his left arm.

Wolf felt waves of prickly pain travel up his arm, and he gritted his teeth and tried to roll to his stomach, but all he could do in the confined space of the doorway was flop around, shifting his body weight up and down on his broken limb, which only made things worse.

"Ah!" he gasped, and he heard Brady making the same noises a few feet away.

Someone stepped close and picked Wolf up by his arms, and Wolf fought back the urge to vomit.

"My sister's up there!" the little girl yelled. "She's up there! The remote control opens up the room!"

Wolf shook his head and tried to concentrate on Elizabeth. Then he watched Burton as he ran inside and picked up the remote. He held it up and examined it for everyone to see. It was a black remote with dark-gray rubber number buttons and a red power button in the upper corner—no different from a basic television remote control.

"Unlock him!" Burton said, pointing at Wolf.

Kazinsky unlocked the handcuffs.

The metal confines clicked and released, and his hands swung down to his sides, sending a fresh wave of pain into his right forearm.

Wolf looked at Elizabeth. "Do you know how to open it?"

"No." Tears were streaming down her face now. "I think he already pushed the button! The door is in the closet!"

"Get her up here!" Wolf yelled as took the steps three at a time. At the top of the stairs he paused and turned around.

Connell was holding the girl under her armpits and racing up behind him; a train of everyone else followed closely.

Wolf ran back down the hall and into the room.

"There," the girl was saying, "in the closet. In the closet!"

Burton swung open the closet door. It was small inside, full of children's clothing on hangars. Otherwise there was nothing—nothing on the floor or on the shelf above.

"Get the clothes out of there," Wolf said.

Burton started ripping the small clothing off the rack and tossing it behind him.

A few seconds later he exposed the rear wall, which was smooth and white, like it had been freshly painted. On the right wall was a keypad—a silver square, mounted flush with white buttons with numbers, like a touch-tone phone. In the lower right of the pad was an enter key.

"Shit," Burton said. "It's a keypad."

"Do you know the combination?" Wolf asked Elizabeth.

She shook her head and started crying harder.

"Heads up," Wolf said, and Kazinsky stepped aside as Wolf pushed his way into the closet.

Burton had his flashlight pulled and was shining it on the pad.

"Let me see that," Wolf said.

"The one and zero," Burton said.

Wolf saw what he meant. The one and zero were clearly dirtier than the other numbers.

"Ten?" Burton asked. "Zero-one? It can only be two combinations." He pecked the keyboard and pushed the enter button after each combination.

Nothing.

"It's one-zero-one," Wolf said.

Burton put in the combination and pressed enter. The entire rear wall clicked open along the edge.

Burton pushed and it didn't move; then he planted his other hand and pushed harder. The wall swung inward, frustratingly slow, so Wolf drove his shoulder into it to help.

As the door swung open, Wolf saw that the frame of the door was constructed of gray stacked cinderblocks, and by the weight they were pushing, the door felt like solid iron or concrete.

Burton snaked inside and Wolf followed as close as he could without tripping him from behind.

A few steps in, Burton came to a stop and Wolf slammed into Burton's back with his forehead.

"Shit," Burton gasped.

Wolf stepped around Burton to see.

Heavy drapes hung over the window so that it was dim inside, but they could still clearly see a small girl right in front of them. Smaller than Elizabeth, she looked no older than five or six.

She was tied to a four-post single bed, with leather cuffs strapped to her wrists and ankles. Braided cables were wound around the leather and extended out like taut guitar strings, where they went to the four posts of the bed and wound into pulley wheels.

As Wolf got closer, the girl's wet, half-closed eyes tracked his, and he knew it was the same girl from the window. She whimpered, barely any sound escaping the red ball gag strapped over her mouth.

Wolf jolted as he realized the whining noise they'd been hearing was mechanical, and the pulley wheels on each post were in fact winches, like the kind he'd seen on the front of ATVs.

"Shoot the cables!"

Burton didn't hesitate. He pulled his pistol and pressed the muzzle against the cable that held a leg.

With a deafening pop the gun flashed and her leg dropped to the bed.

Wolf's hearing muted for a second, but he swore he heard the girl scream, like her pain had suddenly doubled. The winch that was pulling on her leg, now free of tension, turned fast as it flapped the frayed cable against the mattress.

The girl rolled her eyes until only the whites showed.

Without hesitation, Burton shot the other cable.

Her other leg dropped, and then she looked like she was shrinking back to her normal size as her legs traveled up the bed. But it was an optical illusion, because she was being dragged up the mattress to the other two winches.

"Press the power button on the remote!" Wolf yelled, barely hearing his own voice over the ringing in his ears. "Press the power button!"

Burton lined up the muzzle over another of the cables but stopped short of shooting when the winches went quiet.

CHAPTER 5

WOLF SAT in Sheriff Burton's office, trying to ignore the aching itch underneath the cast on his forearm. He dug his index finger inside the top and scratched, feeling a drop of sweat trickle down into the cast. Another drop of sweat trickled out of his armpit and along the inside of his bicep.

A fan hummed and clicked as it swiveled back and forth, offering no comfort against the oppressive heat of Burton's office. The first real hot air of the year was blowing in from the south and into Rocky Points, and it was apparently making its way through the shoddy seals of Burton's window. Or he had the heat on. Either way, it felt like Afghanistan in July.

Burton's flannel swayed on the coat rack, and Wolf caught another whiff of stale cigarette smoke. Burton wore the shirt every time he smoked outside the station garage; even on a day like today, when it was ninety degrees with no clouds, he would have been wearing it. According to Tammy, it was Burton's way to block the smell from seeping into his uniform, which would have tipped off Mrs. Burton when the sheriff got home.

"Then get it to me this afternoon!" Burton's voice bellowed from the hallway.

Wolf stood up and faced the door as it opened.

"Sit, Jesus Christ. Sit." Burton waved his hand and walked around his desk. He sat down with a sigh and pulled on his uniform. "Hot as shit in here. I swear I'm gonna arrest the owner of that air-conditioning company, bring in the contractor who put in these windows, and make them fight to the death in a jail cell."

Wolf sat and pulled at his uniform, too, daydreaming of the SUV's air conditioner drying the crevices of his body.

"Thanks for coming in to talk to me, Wolf." Burton looked him in the eye with genuine gratitude.

Wolf nodded.

"I just wanted to let you know"—he leaned forward on his elbows and hardened his gaze—"that I'm damn proud of what you did last week."

Wolf nodded again. "Thank you, sir."

Burton shook his head. "Shit, you're a man of few words, aren't you?"

Wolf felt his face flush.

"I mean it," Burton said. "Proud. I felt vindicated for believing in you, and then you stepping up so big. And I don't think there's any doubt over your abilities now, not from anyone on this force, and certainly not from me."

Wolf took a breath and glanced out the window beyond Burton.

Burton leaned back and sighed.

"What's the final count?" Wolf asked.

Burton closed his eyes and exhaled through his nose. "They're saying seven. Two boys and five girls."

Wolf felt a glob of molten lead hit his stomach.

By the time Wolf had caught a lucky glimpse of Teresa VKazinsky pleading from behind a quadruple-paned window, she and her older sister, Megan (not Elizabeth), had been missing for three days, taken from outside their home in Casper, Wyoming.

At some point in the past, Brady had found time between running two local businesses, along with a sick desire, to construct the hidden room where they'd found Teresa bound and gagged. Floors soundproofed with rubber padding, walls lined with a foot of cement, and a ceiling made of thick plaster, tack on the window's quadruple panes with thick sheets of bullet-proof glass, and it was an inescapable room for a man with a box of grenades, much less a helpless child.

Forensic analysts had found trace evidence of more children having been in Brady's home. Then the dogs found bones buried in the forest behind James Brady's house. And then they found more.

James Brady, it seemed, had been something much more than a local business owner.

"They got em' all identified," Burton said. "Thomas Quinlan. He was the earliest. Went missing in Provo in eighty-three."

Wolf narrowed his eyes, but said nothing. He never wanted to speak about the guy again.

Burton slapped his hand on the desk. "The important thing is that this fucker's done."

Wolf blinked, trying to think of anything else.

They sat in respectful silence for a minute.

"You know, your dad was just like you in his early twenties," Burton said.

Wolf narrowed his eyes.

"Had a good head. Took charge of situations."

Wolf said nothing.

Burton looked at the ceiling and scratched his chin. "Never pulled his gun on a kid shootin' BBs at pop cans, though."

Wolf clamped his lips in a tight line.

Burton chuckled and then frowned. "I've been meaning to ask you for a week now. How the hell did you know it was one-zero-one on that keypad?"

"Brady said he was at Hamburger Hill in Vietnam. That battle was part of an operation called Apache Snow, which was fought by three airborne infantry battalions from the 101st Airborne Division, sir."

Burton stared at Wolf for a few seconds and then raised his eyebrows. "Anyways, I've officially taken you off the shitlist, and put you on the watch-list."

"Thank ... you?" Wolf had no idea what that meant.

"You're welcome." Burton waved his hand and looked at a piece of paper at his desk.

Wolf scooted his chair back and stood up.

"When's that thing come off?" Burton pointed at Wolf's cast and then picked up his desk phone.

"Six weeks, sir."

Burton dialed the phone and twisted in his chair toward the window.

Wolf stood for another few seconds and then let himself out.

The temperature dropped at least ten degrees as he left Burton's office. Kazinsky was in the hallway, talking with Deputy Connell next to the water cooler.

"So?" Kazinsky asked in a voice barely above a whisper. "How'd it go?"

Connell threw the water in his mouth, tossed the cup in the trash and walked away toward the squad room.

Wolf pinched a cone of paper from the dispenser and filled it up. He sucked it down, and the ice-cold liquid splashed in his stomach, making him feel like he'd been hit in the gut with a snowball. He crumpled the cup and tossed it in the trash.

"Let's get back to work," Wolf said.

THE END.

David Wolf Series in Order

Gut Decision (A David Wolf Short Story)
    Foreign Deceit (Wolf #1) **Free at Amazon
    The Silversmith (Wolf #2)
    Alive and Killing (Wolf #3)
    Deadly Conditions (Wolf #4)
    Cold Lake (Wolf #5)
    Smoked Out (Wolf #6)

To the Bone (Wolf #7)
Dire (Wolf #8)
Signature (Wolf #9)

Sign up for the newsletter to stay up to date with new books at jeffcarson.co/p/newsletter.html.

DAVID WOLF SERIES IN ORDER

Made in the USA
Middletown, DE
03 September 2024

60124869R00031